SORRY!

BY
TRUDY LUDWIG

ILLUSTRATIONS BY
MAURIE J. MANNING

Tricycle Press
Berkeley

My friend Charlie is always doing stuff he shouldn't. And he gets away with it—even when he does it on purpose. Like the time he took his sister Anna's favorite school picture and drew a mustache on it.

"CHARLIE!" his mom screeched. "You say you're sorry to Anna . . . **RIGHT THIS INSTANT!**"

And Charlie did what he was told. But I could tell he didn't mean it. So could Anna.

"Now Anna, what do you say to your brother?" their mom asked.

A tear dropped onto the ruined photo Anna held in her hands.

"Honey, you need to forgive him."

Anna looked at Charlie. He grinned back. That's when Anna started to bawl even harder. She ran to her room and slammed the door.

Charlie turned to his mom. "Geez, I said I was sorry. What's her problem?"

"Jack, did you see what happened here between Charlie and Anna?" Charlie's mom asked me.

I shrugged. I wasn't about to say anything. No way.

Before I met Charlie, I was a nobody. The one the other kids ordered to "move over!" in the cafeteria. The first one ignored in class and the last one picked for teams at recess.

Then I was a somebody. I was Charlie's friend. I lucked into being his friend when I rescued Charlie's Frisbee from Mr. Finkelstein's roof. Charlie thought it was pretty cool that I didn't get caught.

Being friends with Charlie wasn't easy. He wanted me to do things I didn't feel comfortable doing.

"What are you, a goody-goody?" he'd say. "Besides, it's no big deal, Jack. If you get caught, just say you're sorry."

I had to admit it sounded easy enough. And I was worried that if I didn't do what Charlie wanted, I'd end up being a nobody again.

So one Saturday, I decided to follow Charlie's advice. I'd invited some guys over to toss water balloons in my front yard.

"Think fast!" we'd yell at each other, hoping the balloon would burst when one of us caught it. I had a water balloon in my hand when Charlie spotted my neighbor Mike by his mailbox.

"Toss it to Mike!" said Charlie.

"Think fast!" I shouted as I threw the water balloon at Mike. It was obvious he wouldn't be able to catch it, but I threw it anyway. The balloon burst when it hit Mike in the chest.

"Bull's eye!" said Charlie, and the other guys cracked up.

"Hah, hah. Very funny," said Mike, all red in the face.

"Sorry Mike!" I called back.

"Yeah, right," he muttered as he walked up his driveway.

I thought saying sorry would make me feel better. But it didn't. I felt even worse because Mike and I both knew that I'd thrown the water balloon at him on purpose.

A few weeks later, Charlie and I went to the auditorium to watch kids set up their displays for the science fair. Charlie noticed Leena putting together her styrofoam solar system. He nudged me in the ribs and headed in her direction. "This is not good," I thought as I followed.

Leena, you see, was my friend—at least she was until Charlie came along. I stopped hanging out with her because it didn't look good to be friends with a brainiac girl. I knew this hurt Leena's feelings, but a guy's gotta do what a guy's gotta do to be cool—right?

THE SUN

Mars
The Red Plan

"Is this a solar system you're making?" asked Charlie as he fingered the styrofoam balls on the table.

Leena nodded and kept working on her project.

"Wow—these balls are really light," said Charlie as he grabbed three and started juggling with them.

"Leave those alone!" said Leena. "You'll wreck them!"

Charlie ignored her and continued to juggle. Leena looked at me. I knew she was hoping I'd say or do something to stop Charlie. But I just stood there, watching.

Suddenly Charlie tossed all three balls high up into the air and shouted "Hey, Jack—catch!"

I tried to catch all of them. I really did. But I could only catch one. The other two hit the floor and didn't look so good.

"You did that on purpose!" Leena yelled at Charlie. "And you let him!" she added, pointing at me.

"Sorry!" we both said.

"Sorry doesn't cut it!" she snapped back.

Mr. Marcus, the science teacher, came over to see what the commotion was about. "What's going on here?" he asked.

"They were messing around with my science project and ruined it!" said Leena.

"We were just having some fun, and we already told her we were sorry . . . right, Jack?"

Mr. Marcus looked at me but I couldn't look him in the eyes. I just stared at my sneakers and wished I were anywhere else.

"Jack, what do you think Leena's feeling right now about what you did?" Mr. Marcus asked me.

I looked at Leena and said in a small voice what I saw on her face: "Really mad . . . and sad."

"Are you truly sorry, boys?" Mr. Marcus asked.

"Like I said, we told her we were sorry," said Charlie.

"Then show it."

"What?"

"Show Leena you're sorry by making right your wrong."

Charlie stood there, looking confused. I got the feeling Mr. Marcus was the first person who ever expected more than a "Sorry!" from him.

It was obvious Charlie didn't know what to do. But I did: "Leena, we're really sorry for ruining your science project." Then I turned to Charlie. "C'mon, let's go to the art room and get some more styrofoam, glue, and paint."

It took us a while to fix the mess we'd made of Leena's planets.

"Man—this is a lot of work," said Charlie as he put the finishing touches of color on Mars.

"I know," said Leena.

Charlie was quiet after that. When we were finally done, Charlie asked if I wanted to shoot some hoops with him and the other guys.

"No thanks," I said. "I'm gonna stick around and help Leena clean up."

She smiled. That's when I knew Leena believed I was sorry for what I did.

"Hey Leena . . . "

"What?"

"I think your project is out of this world!"

She rolled her eyes. "C'mon wise guy," she said. "I'll race you to the snack bar. Loser buys . . . deal?"

"Deal!"

Afterword

An apology is one of the most profound interactions between individuals, groups, and nations. It has the power to undo the shame and guilt of the offending party. It can dissolve grudges and vengeance and forge harmony in the relationship. Without an apology, there may be no forgiveness.

In order to understand why some apologies heal while others hurt, it can be useful to first look at the four parts of an apology: acknowledging the offense, offering an explanation, expressing shame and remorse, and offering reparation. When an apology fails, at least one of these four parts is missing or inadequate. The most common failing is *inadequately acknowledging the offense*, such as: "I am sorry for whatever I did," "Mistakes were made," "If I upset you, I am sorry," "What I did was trivial but I am sorry for what I did." *Ineffective explanations* can cause an apology to fail, such as "someone else made me do it" or "I was just trying to get even." *Insincere expressions of remorse* can cause an apology to fail, such as "I'm sorry" when the true meaning is "I am sorry I was caught." Finally, *inadequate reparations* can cause an apology to fail when it is clear that repair of psychological or physical damage could make the offended party whole.

How do these four parts of an apology heal or mend the broken relationship? They may heal because the offender validated the offended party's experience and acknowledged that the offense was not the offended party's fault. They may heal because the offender has restored the dignity of the person who was hurt. They may heal because the offender showed the victim that they also suffered. They may heal because the offender restored the material damage that resulted. Of all these ways of healing, the most common mechanism of "cure" is the restoration of dignity.

Making a genuine apology seems like a sensible, constructive thing to do when one person offends another. Yet it is remarkable how frequently apologies are withheld or offered in a manner that offends rather than heals. The reasons for such failures are the fear of being shamed, being seen as weak, being rejected, or the like. With fears like these, we can see that learning to apologize is no small matter. Overcoming them requires honesty, generosity, commitment, humility, and courage.

Apologizing is best learned in childhood and the most obvious teachers are parents and educators. Yet when we adults are clumsy and fearful about apologizing, when we believe it is dangerous to apologize, when we believe apologizing is a sign of weakness, we are apt to fail as positive role models for our children.

Parents who are comfortable with apologizing can teach this important skill to their children by making appropriate apologies to their children, or by letting them observe how grownups effectively apologize to each other. The child will see that no one is hurt, no one is humiliated, relationships are restored, and love is preserved.

Trudy Ludwig's wonderful book, *Sorry!*, helps parents and educators teach children the magic transformative power of apology. The seemingly simple story in this book has many lessons to teach. The first is how an offender can feel shame (and possibly guilt) over his or her offense. The second is that the simple phrase "I'm sorry" is rarely an effective apology. No quick fix. The third is that it is important for the offender to acknowledge the offense so both parties know what the apology is for. The fourth is that reparations are necessary to restore the damage and communicate caring and respect for the victim. The fifth is that the person who apologizes can be relieved of shame and guilt. The sixth is that the relationship between the offender and the victim is restored and even strengthened. Finally, we see that it takes courage on the part of the offender to do the right thing, even at the risk of losing another relationship. Such a seemingly simple apology does so much, and Trudy Ludwig captures its essence in a manner that will touch the heart of parent and child alike.

Aaron Lazare, M.D., dean, chancellor, and professor of psychiatry, University of Massachusetts Medical School, and author of *On Apology*

A Note from the Author: Apologies from the Heart

In my efforts to referee hurt feelings I, too, have been guilty of telling my children: "Say you're sorry . . . RIGHT NOW!" I remember one particular occasion when my child's apology was so blatantly insincere that even I couldn't help but be offended by it. That's when it dawned on me how destructive an insincere apology can be, adding further insult to the already injured party.

An insincere apology reflects an intentional disregard of—and contempt for—another's feelings. It also shows the lack of personal responsibility and remorse for the hurtful misdeed.

Forcing children to say they're sorry when they don't mean it, or pressuring children to accept apologies that ring false, does more harm than good. Both parties need to process what happened: the wrongdoers to figure out how to show genuine remorse by making right their wrongs; and the targets to work through their feelings of hurt and anger so they can embrace apologies from the heart.

How can we guide our children in the art of making a sincere apology? According to Dr. Aaron Lazare, a leading expert on this subject and the author of *On Apology*, simply saying "sorry" is not enough to repair the damage done by the wrongdoer. Being specific about the hurt one has caused another ("I am very sorry I drew on your picture and ruined it"), asking for the injured party's input ("what can I do to show you how badly I feel and make things better between us?"), and replacing or repairing damaged items are some ways to show sincere regret and make amends. Beverly Engel, renowned therapist and author of *The Power of Apology*, sums up a meaningful apology best when she describes it as being comprised of the three R's: Regret, Responsibility, and Remedy.

By helping children comprehend the implications of their hurtful behaviors and take responsibility for their actions, we foster a future where empathy and understanding—not hate or distrust—prevail.

Trudy Ludwig

Questions for Discussion

"I said I was sorry!"

Which do you think is worse: Charlie drawing a mustache on Anna's favorite school picture or Charlie saying sorry to his sister and not meaning it?

How can you tell when someone says he or she is sorry and really means it?

What do you think Charlie could have done to convince his sister that he was genuinely sorry?

What could Jack have done or said to show Mike he was truly sorry for throwing a water balloon at him?

Have you ever been forced to say you're sorry when you don't mean it? Give an example.

Have you ever been forced to accept someone's apology when you're still really mad and aren't ready to forgive? Give an example.

People make mistakes—sometimes by accident, sometimes on purpose. What would it take for you to genuinely forgive them?

"A guy's gotta do what a guy's gotta do to be cool."

Why do you think Jack agreed to throw a water balloon at his neighbor Mike, even though he knew it was the wrong thing to do?

What makes a boy popular at your school? What makes a girl popular?

What are the advantages of being popular? What are the disadvantages?

Do you think kids who are popular can more easily get away with doing mean things compared to those kids who aren't? Explain.

What kind of qualities do you look for in a good friend?

"I knew she was hoping I'd say or do something to stop Charlie. But I just stood there . . ."

Jack knew Charlie was going to make a mess of Leena's science project. Why do you think he didn't stop him?

Do you think Leena was right to place equal blame on Jack and Charlie for ruining her science project? Why or why not?

What could Jack have said or done to prevent Leena's project from being destroyed by Charlie?

What would you do if you saw a friend saying or doing something hurtful to another friend?

Apology Dos & Don'ts

Apologies have the power to heal the human spirit, open the heart to forgiveness, and restore relationships. Just as every child is unique, so is the apology he or she makes. According to Dr. Lazare, some apologies may require all of these suggestions to be effective, while others may not.

Do:

✳ Be sincere. A false apology can be more harmful than no apology at all.

✳ Look the person you've hurt in the eye and openly admit what you've done wrong.

✳ Let the person you've hurt know that he or she did nothing wrong.

✳ Allow the person you've harmed to share his or her feelings of hurt, anger, and discomfort with you. Be a good listener.

✳ Make the effort to right your wrong. For example, write a letter, draw a picture, or replace or repair a damaged item. If necessary, ask the person for suggestions. If you can't agree to a solution, ask a grown-up for help.

✳ Let the person you've hurt know that you won't repeat what you did and keep your promise.

Don't:

✳ Simply say "I'm sorry" or "I apologize" without being specific about what you've done wrong.

✳ Make excuses for your wrongdoings. Take responsibility for your words and behavior.

✳ Be afraid to let the other person know how badly you feel about what you've done. The person you've hurt wants to know that you have suffered as well.

✳ Expect others to forgive you right away if they're still working through their feelings of hurt, anger, and pain.

✳ Let others apologize for your misdeed. Make the apology yourself.

✳ Think it's too late to apologize. Apologies from the heart can heal old hurts.

TRUDY LUDWIG
Making a Difference in Kids' Lives, One Book at a Time®

Children's advocate and author Trudy Ludwig has received rave reviews nationwide from educators, experts, organizations, and parents for her passion and compassion in addressing relational aggression—the use of relationships to manipulate and hurt others. Trudy wrote her first book, *My Secret Bully*, after her own daughter was bullied by friends. Since then she has become a sought-after speaker, visiting schools around the country and educating students, parents, and teachers on the topic.

Just Kidding takes a look at emotional bullying among boys who use biting humor in hurtful ways, and *Trouble Talk* uncovers the harmful consequences of gossiping, spreading rumors, and sharing others' information in order to establish connection and gain attention.

Trudy lives in Portland, Oregon, with her husband and two children. For more information or to book Trudy for your school or conference, visit www.trudyludwig.com.

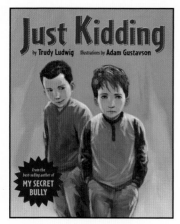

ISBN-13: 978-1-58246-163-2
ISBN-10: 1-58246-163-5
Also available in Spanish

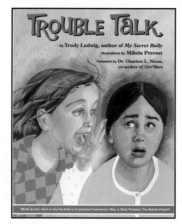

ISBN-13: 978-1-58246-240-0
ISBN-10: 1-58246-240-2

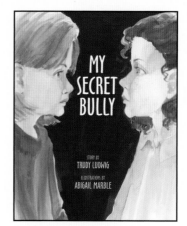

ISBN-13: 978-1-58246-159-5
ISBN-10: 1-58246-159-7
Also available in Spanish

"*Just Kidding* is an outstanding resource for parents and educators to empower children with important coping skills. A wonderful addition to school libraries."

—Judy S. Freedman, M.S.W., L.C.S.W., author of *Easing the Teasing: Helping Your Child Cope with Name-Calling, Ridicule, and Verbal Bullying*

"The story expands our understanding of a 'bully' from the boy in the schoolyard who steals your lunch money—to a person who might be your best friend."

—Rachel Simmons, author of *Odd Girl Out*

For Judy, Craig, Alice, Susan, and Kirk. –T.J.L.

For Robin and Dani. –M.J.M.

Text copyright © 2006 by Trudy Ludwig
Illustrations copyright © 2006 by Maurie J. Manning

All rights reserved. Published in the United States by Tricycle Press, an imprint of Random House Children's Books, a division of Random House, Inc., New York.
www.randomhouse.com/kids

Tricycle Press and the Tricycle Press colophon are registered trademarks of Random House, Inc.

Library of Congress Cataloging-in-Publication Data
Ludwig, Trudy.
Sorry! / by Trudy Ludwig ; illustrations by Maurie Manning.
p. cm.
Summary: When Jack makes friends with Charlie, a trouble-maker, he learns the difference between an insincere apology and showing that you are truly sorry. Includes information for parents.
[1. Apologizing--Fiction. 2. Behavior--Fiction.] I. Manning, Maurie, ill.
II. Title.
PZ7.L9763So 2006
[E]--dc22
                    2006005761

ISBN 978-1-58246-173-1

Printed in China

Design by Randall Heath
Typeset in CG Symphony and Burghley
The illustrations in this book were rendered using Corel Painter IX
in digital pastel and watercolor.

16 - 20

First Edition